Dark Man

How many have you read?

Dark Man

The Bridge of Dark Tears
by Peter Lancett
illustrated by Jan Pedroietta

Published by Ransom Publishing Ltd.
Radley House, 8 St. Cross Road, Winchester, Hampshire, UK
SO23 9HX
www.ransom.co.uk

ISBN   978 184167 746 0

First published in 2011

Dark Man

The Bridge of Dark Tears

by Peter Lancett

illustrated by Jan Pedroietta

Ransom

Chapter One:
Beautiful but Sad

A river runs through the city.

The waters are black and thick with waste.

Late one night, a girl waits alone on a bridge that crosses the river.

The girl is called Josie.

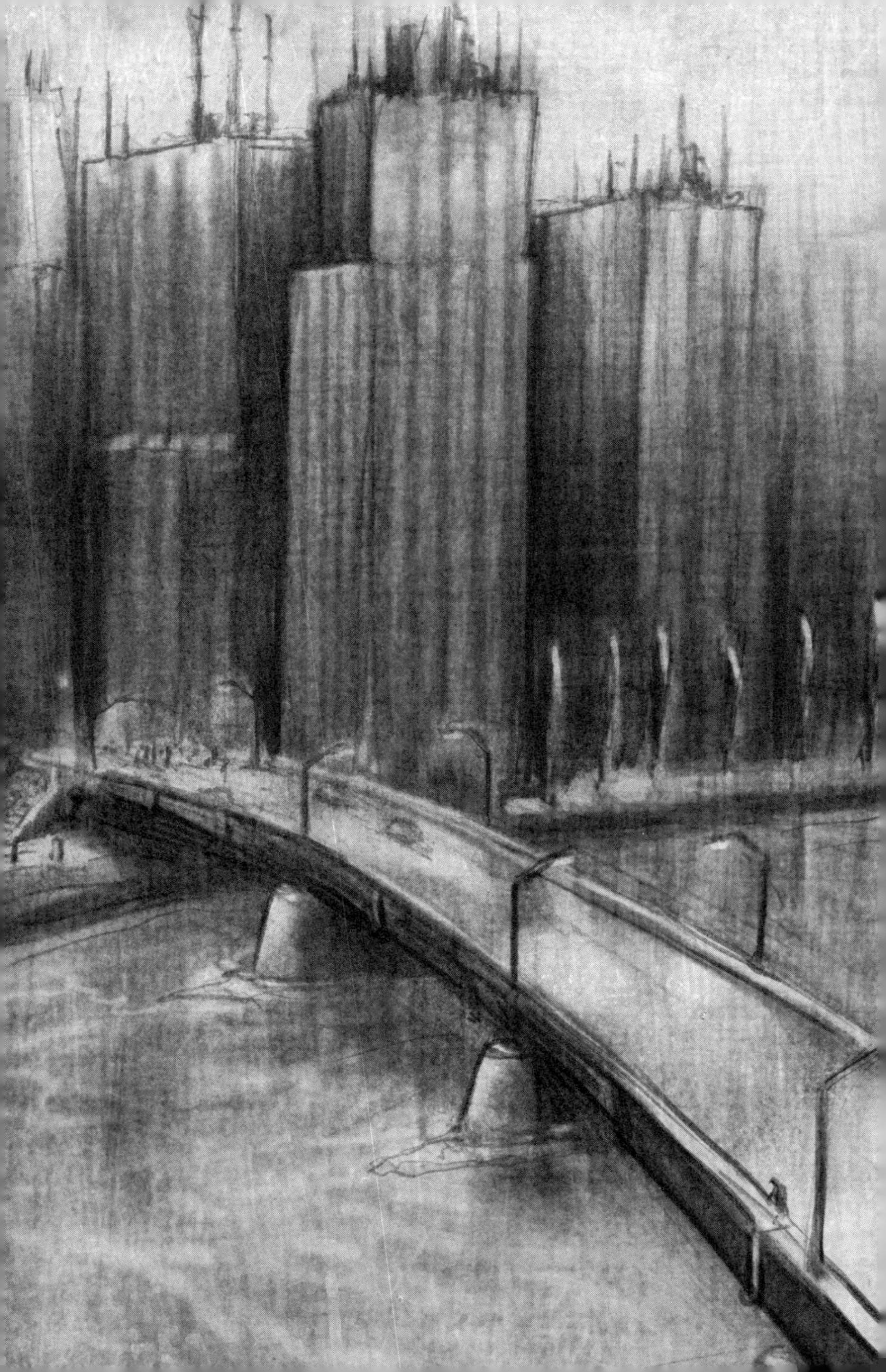

She is beautiful, but she is always sad.

Tonight, she is waiting for the Dark Man.

As she looks down into the poisoned water, a voice comes from behind her.

'The Old Man told me that I would find you here. You must be Josie.'

Josie turns to see the Dark Man.

'I did not hear your footsteps,' she says.

The Dark Man smiles. 'It pays to move quietly after dark.'

Josie nods.

'The Old Man has asked me to help you. He thinks that I can find something that most people cannot see.'

The Dark Man sees the sadness in Josie's eyes.

'The Old Man is usually right about such things,'
he says.

He takes Josie by the hand.

'Come on,' he says. 'It will be safer to look during the day.'

Chapter Two:
By the River

Next day, the Dark Man and Josie are walking along the riverbank.

Josie looks down into the water.

'What would happen if you fell in?' she asks.

The Dark Man shakes his head.

'Even if you did not drown, you would soon die. There are poisons in the water.'

Josie nods, and they continue to walk.

'What does the Old Man want me to find?' she asks.

'A bridge,' the Dark Man tells her.

'But a bridge is big. Anyone can see a bridge.'

On the far side of the river, there are glittering buildings. It is the good part of the city.

There are people in smart clothes sitting at café tables.

The Dark Man points at them.

'**They** would never see it,' he says.

In the late afternoon, the Dark Man and Josie
rest by the side of the river.

'Why are you always sad?' the Dark Man asks.

'I am alone,' Josie tells him. 'Mother, father, sister – all are gone.'

'Lots of people lose their loved ones,' the Dark Man says.

'I did not lose them,' Josie says. 'The Shadow Masters took them.'

The Dark Man thinks of a night long ago, in the heart of a dense forest.

He sees Astrid, a girl that he loves, taken by the Shadow Masters.

He had not been able to help her, and the pain still lives inside him.

The Dark Man takes Josie by the hand, and a smile almost comes to her lips.

Her eyes remain dark with sorrow, but the Dark Man's touch comforts her.

'We should continue,' the Dark Man says. 'It will be night, soon.'

Chapter Three:
Dark Tears

Later, as they walk along the river bank, Josie suddenly stops and gasps.

'What is it?' The Dark Man asks.

'The bridge. Look at it!'

She turns her head, no longer able to face it.

'I see nothing,' the Dark Man says.

'There! Look!' Josie is pointing.

The Dark Man takes her hand, and suddenly he can see what she sees.

There is a bridge of black, crumbling stone.

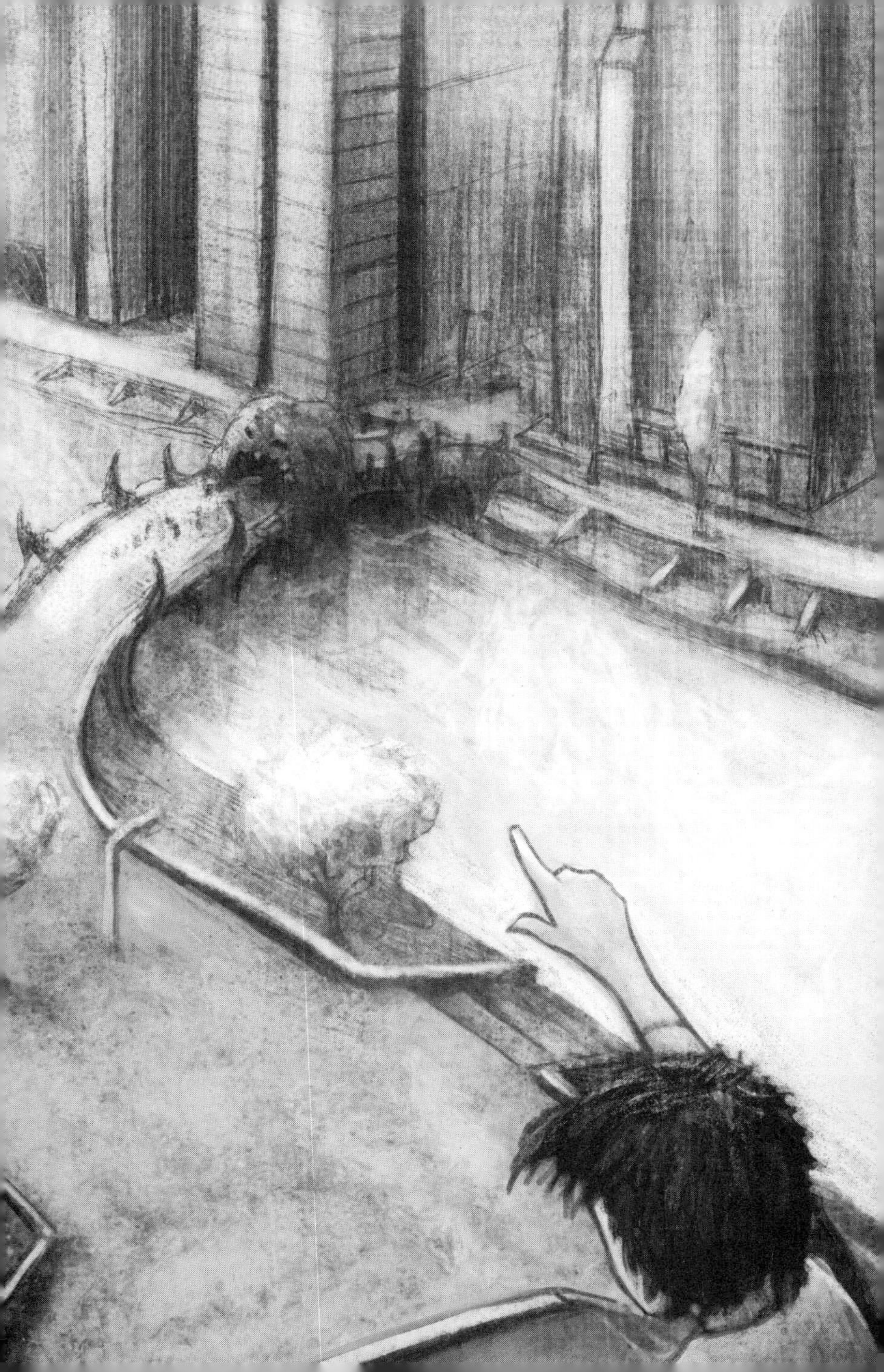

In the middle sits a huge demon head, facing the bad part of the city, its mouth belching fire.

Two Shadow Masters usher sad-faced children into this blazing mouth.

From the underside of the bridge, black liquid drips into the river below, hissing as it hits the poisoned water.

It looks like the bridge is crying dark tears.

Then the Dark Man notices what is happening on the far side of the demon head.

Men and women are emerging from the back of the head.

They look like the people from the good part of the city.

Josie has noticed them too.

'What is happening?' she asks fearfully.

'The Shadow Masters are turning the children into slaves. They are sending them to the good part of the city,' the Dark Man tells her.

'Why?'

'Because these slaves will fit in there. They can work in the daylight, when the Shadow Masters dare not come out.'

Josie is very scared.

'Come,' the Dark Man says. 'You must lead me to the bridge. I cannot see it on my own. We must stop this.'

Josie shakes her head. 'I am afraid,' she says.

But the Dark Man senses courage deep within her.

Together, they walk towards the bridge.

Chapter Four:
Sparkling Light

As they near the bridge, one of the Shadow Masters notices them and cries out.

The Shadow Master waves at the demon head with an open hand.

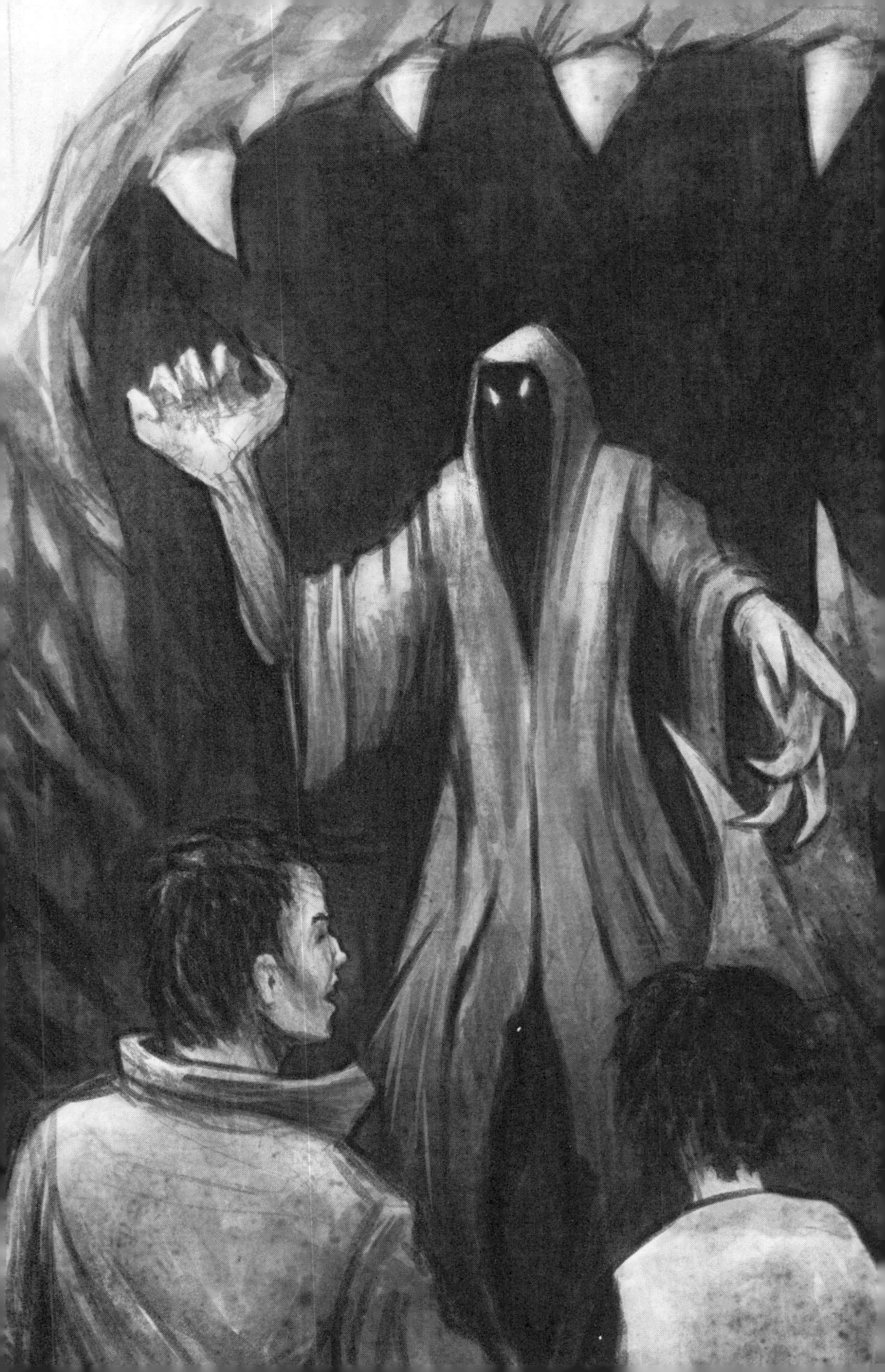

The head's eyes open, glaring at the Dark Man.

It belches a huge flame towards the Dark Man and Josie.

As Josie hides behind him, the Dark Man stands tall.

Sparkling light surrounds him, protecting him. '
deflects the flame down into the waters be'

The sparkling light seems to grow like a mighty angel, a hundred feet high.

In its right hand, this angelic figure carries a shining sword of silver light.

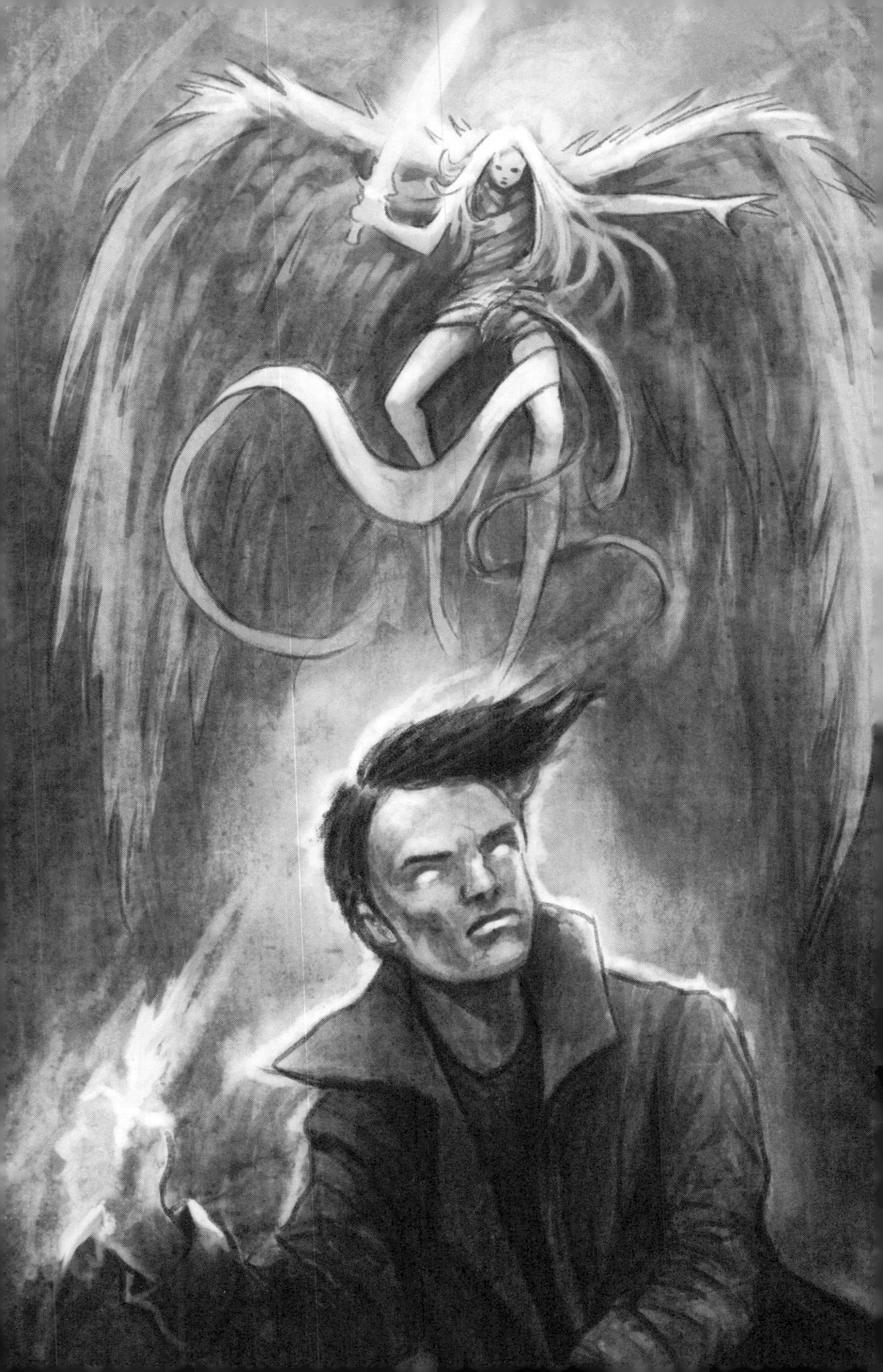

The Dark Man raises his arm, and the sparkling figure raises its own arm, holding the sword high.

The Dark Man brings his arm crashing down and the angelic sword seems to cut the demon head in two.

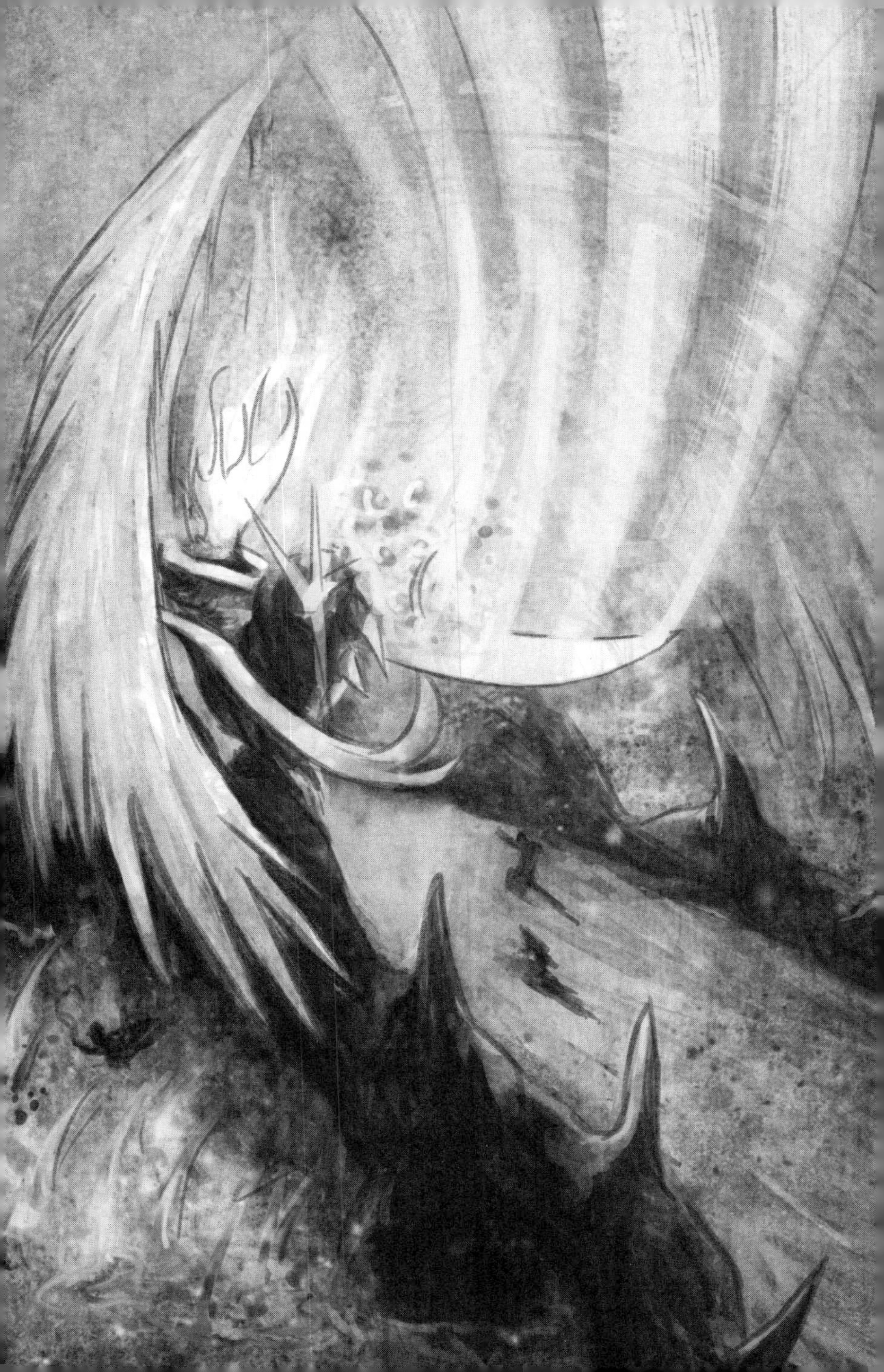

The Shadow Masters scream as the bridge is smashed by the sword of light.

They fall into the poisoned water and never come to the surface.

The dark stones of the bridge begin to shine, as they tumble into the river beneath.

Chapter Four:
Children Again

The Dark Man lies drained at the river's edge.

Josie has crawled to his side.

The figure of light has gone.

And so has the bridge.

Josie shakes the Dark Man's shoulder.

'Look!' she says, pointing at the far river bank.

The Dark Man lifts his head to see.

Scruffy children are wandering around, as though they are lost.

The slaves have become children again.

'We have beaten them,' Josie says.

The Dark Man turns to her.

'For now,' he says.

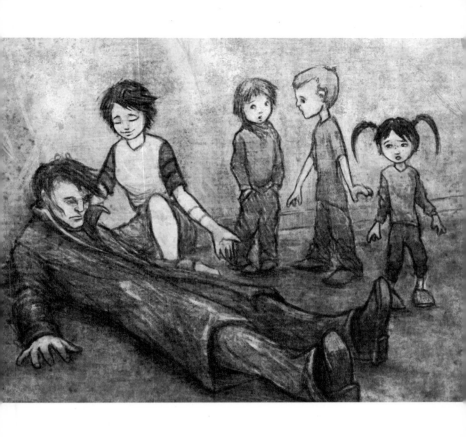

But for the first time, he sees a smile come to her eyes.

The author

Peter Lancett is a writer, editor and film maker. He has written many books, and has just made a feature film, *The Xlitherman*.

Peter now lives in New Zealand and California.